This Little Tiger book belongs to:

To everyone I've ever known
    who's had a bugbear of their own.
From queue-jumpers to summer rain,
    to standing-room only on the train. ~ PH

To Angel, for being there ~ CS

LITTLE TIGER PRESS LTD
an imprint of the Little Tiger Group
1 Coda Studios
189 Munster Road, London SW6 6AW
www.littletiger.co.uk

First published in Great Britain 2017
This edition published 2018
Text by Patricia Hegarty
Text copyright © Little Tiger Press 2017
Illustrations copyright © Carmen Saldaña 2017
Carmen Saldaña has asserted her right
to be identified as the illustrator of this work
under the Copyright, Designs and Patents Act, 1988
A CIP catalogue record for this book
is available from the British Library
All rights reserved

ISBN 978-1-78881-038-8
LTP/1800/2260/0218
Printed in China
10 9 8 7 6 5 4 3 2 1

BUG
BEAR

Patricia Hegarty

Carmen Saldaña

LITTLE TIGER
LONDON

Down in the forest,
    as Bear had a doze,
A small stripy bug
    came and sat on his nose.

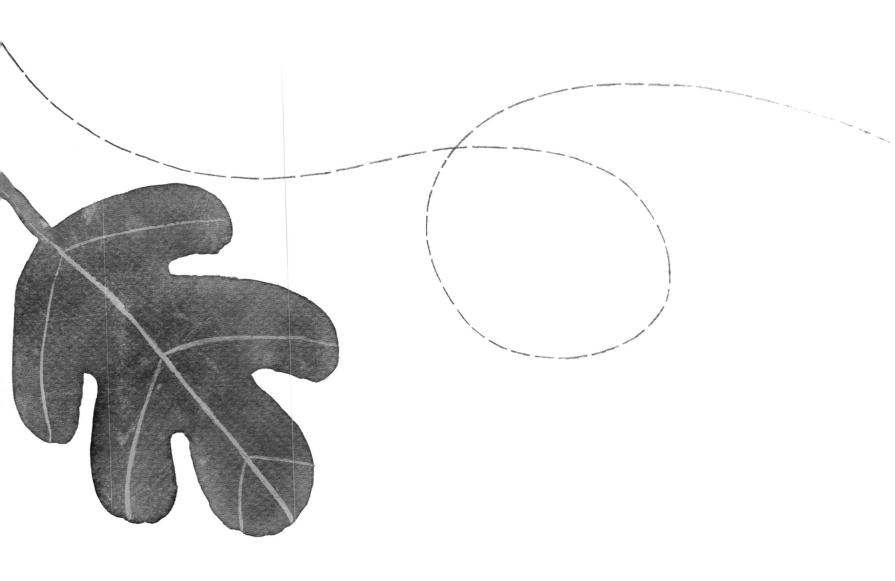

"Good day to you, Bear, I'm just passing through,
Looking for lodgings...
          and I've chosen YOU!"

Bear lifted his head and opened one eye,
Then closed it again with a world-weary sigh.

But Bug wasn't easy
for Bear to ignore.

He whirred
and he buzzed
and then buzzed
a bit more.

"You're lovely and squidgy,
and cuddly, dear Bear —
And you DO have a lot
of that warm fur to spare."

"But your fur is so fuzzy, so soft and so snug –
It's just perfect bedding for a little old bug!"

Bug looped the loop,
then he sat on Bear's snout.
"Come now, my friend, let's both hug it out."

"I don't want to hug you, you fluttering pest.
Why can't you see that I'm trying to REST!"

"You're SO funny, Bear," said Bug with a giggle. And he nestled right down with a jiggly wiggle.

"Stop tickling me, Bug!" said Bear with a snuffle.
"Oh, WHY are you causing this great big kerfuffle?"

Bear hopped and he clopped
and jumped up and down.

He swished and he swatted
then said with a frown...

"Oh, troublesome bug,
why on earth pick on me,
And not one of these other fine
CREATURES you see?"

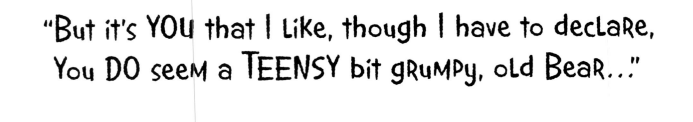

"But it's YOU that I like, though I have to declare,
You DO seem a TEENSY bit grumpy, old Bear..."

"GRUMPY?!" said Bear.
"GRUMPY, you say?!"

"I'll give you grumpy –
you've ruined my day!"

"Won't SOMEBODY
help me?"
cried Bear with a howl.

"Can I be of service?"
called clever old Owl.

"Oh Owl," whimpered Bear,
"please tell him from me,
He's GOT to buzz off and just let me be!"

"Don't worry," said Owl, "for I have a plan.
Bear can't be your bed, but I know who can.
My friend is just perfect, I'm sure you'll agree.
He's soft and he's hanging
up there in that **tree.**"

"Well, why on earth
I'm all ears," said

"Alright," said Owl
Now please sa,

idn't you say so before?
Bug. "You must tell me more!"

don't get in a froth.
ello to my furry friend Sloth."

"I'd be MOST grateful," said Sloth with a grin,
"To have a small bug make his home on my skin.
I don't get about much, because I'm so slow.
Now YOU'LL be my best friend wherever I go!"

More fabulous books from Little Tiger Press!

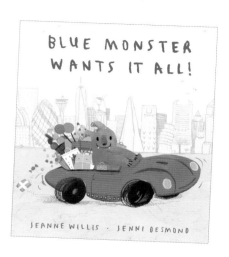

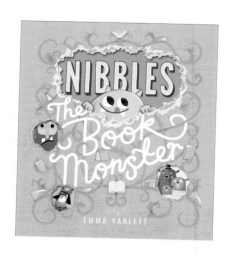

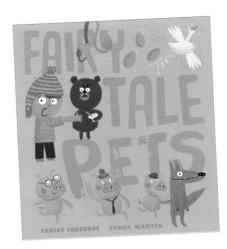

For information regarding any of the above books or for our catalogue, please contact us:
Little Tiger Press, 1 Coda Studios, 189 Munster Road, London SW6 6AW
Tel: 020 7385 6333 • E-mail: contact@littletiger.co.uk • www.littletiger.co.uk